MARVEL

ANT-MAN

By Billy Wrecks
Illustrated by Patrick Spaziante

 A GOLDEN BOOK • NEW YORK

marvelkids.com
© 2016 MARVEL

All rights reserved. Published in the United States by Golden Books, an imprint of
Random House Children's Books, a division of Penguin Random House LLC, 1745 Broadway,
New York, NY 10019, and in Canada by Random House of Canada, a division of Penguin Random House Ltd.,
Toronto. Golden Books, A Golden Book, A Little Golden Book, the G colophon, and the distinctive
gold spine are registered trademarks of Penguin Random House LLC.

randomhousekids.com

Educators and librarians, for a variety of teaching tools, visit us at RHTeachersLibrarians.com

ISBN 978-0-399-55097-3

Printed in the United States of America

10 9 8 7 6 5 4 3 2

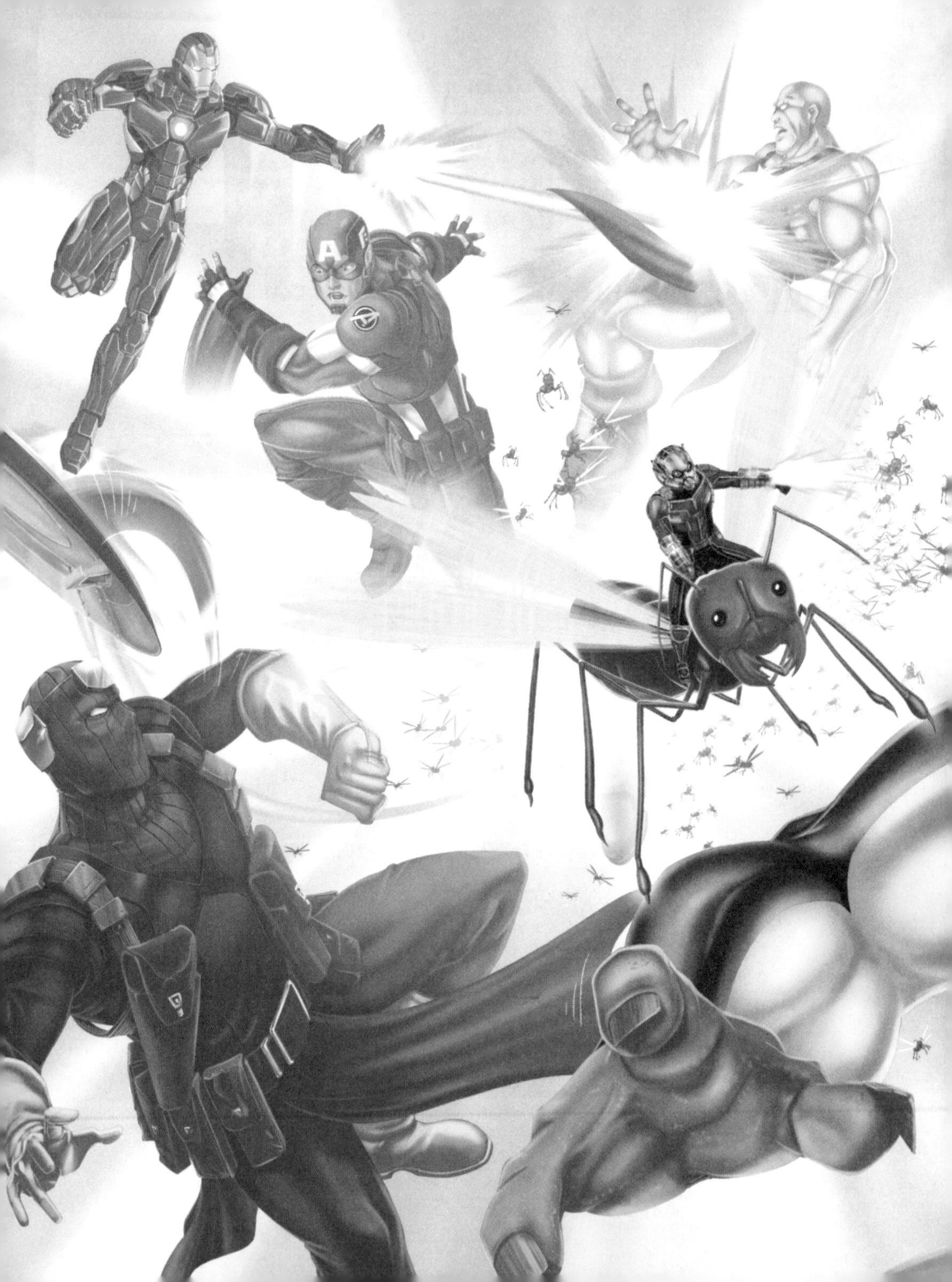

ANT-MAN is the tiniest member of the superhero team known as the **AVENGERS**. But don't let his size fool you—Ant-Man packs a powerful punch!

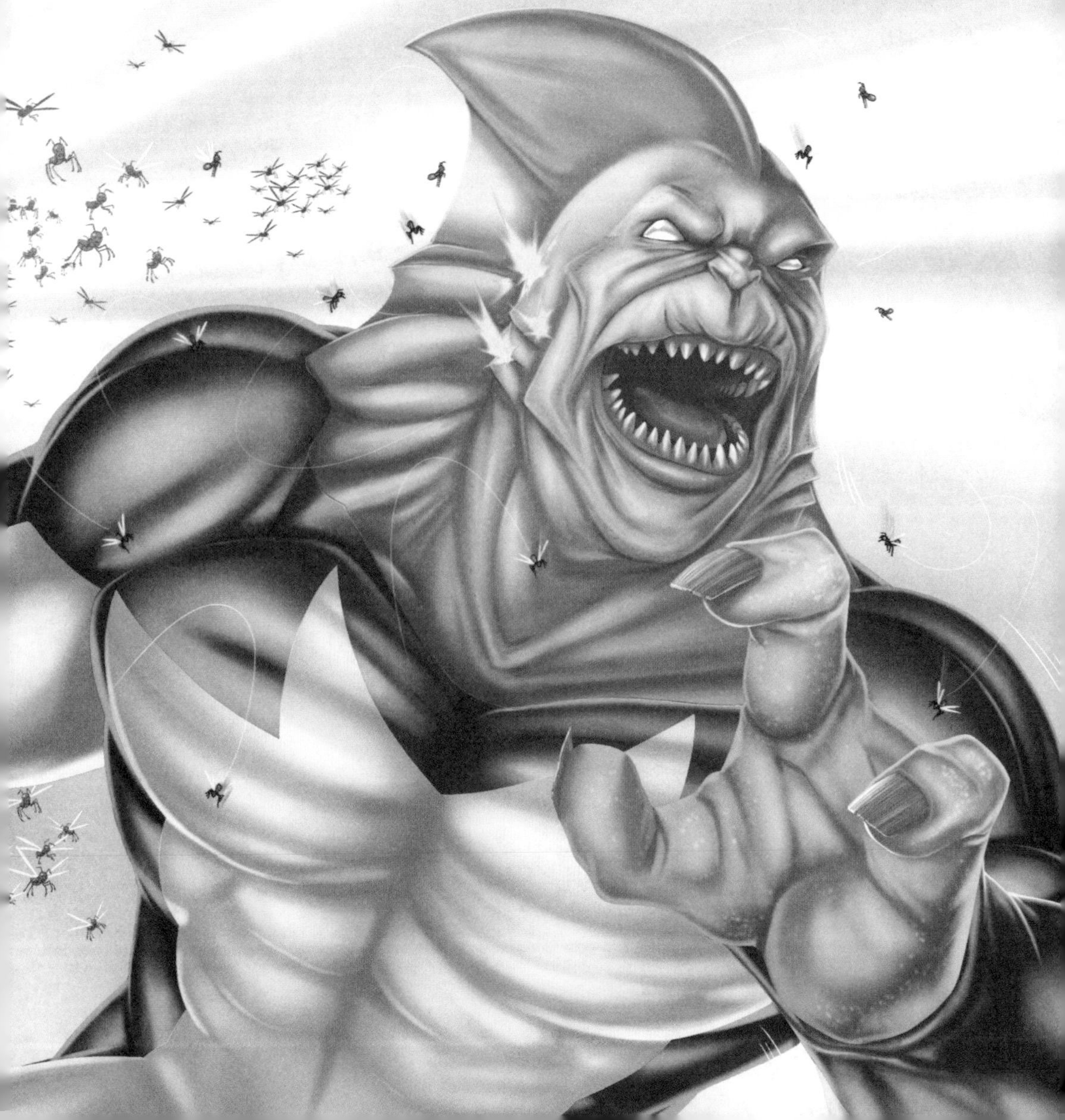

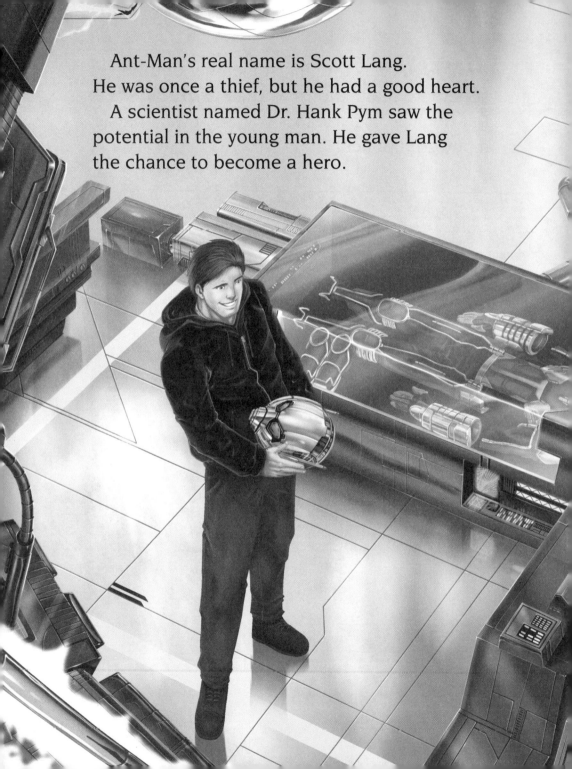

Ant-Man's real name is Scott Lang.
He was once a thief, but he had a good heart.
A scientist named Dr. Hank Pym saw the
potential in the young man. He gave Lang
the chance to become a hero.

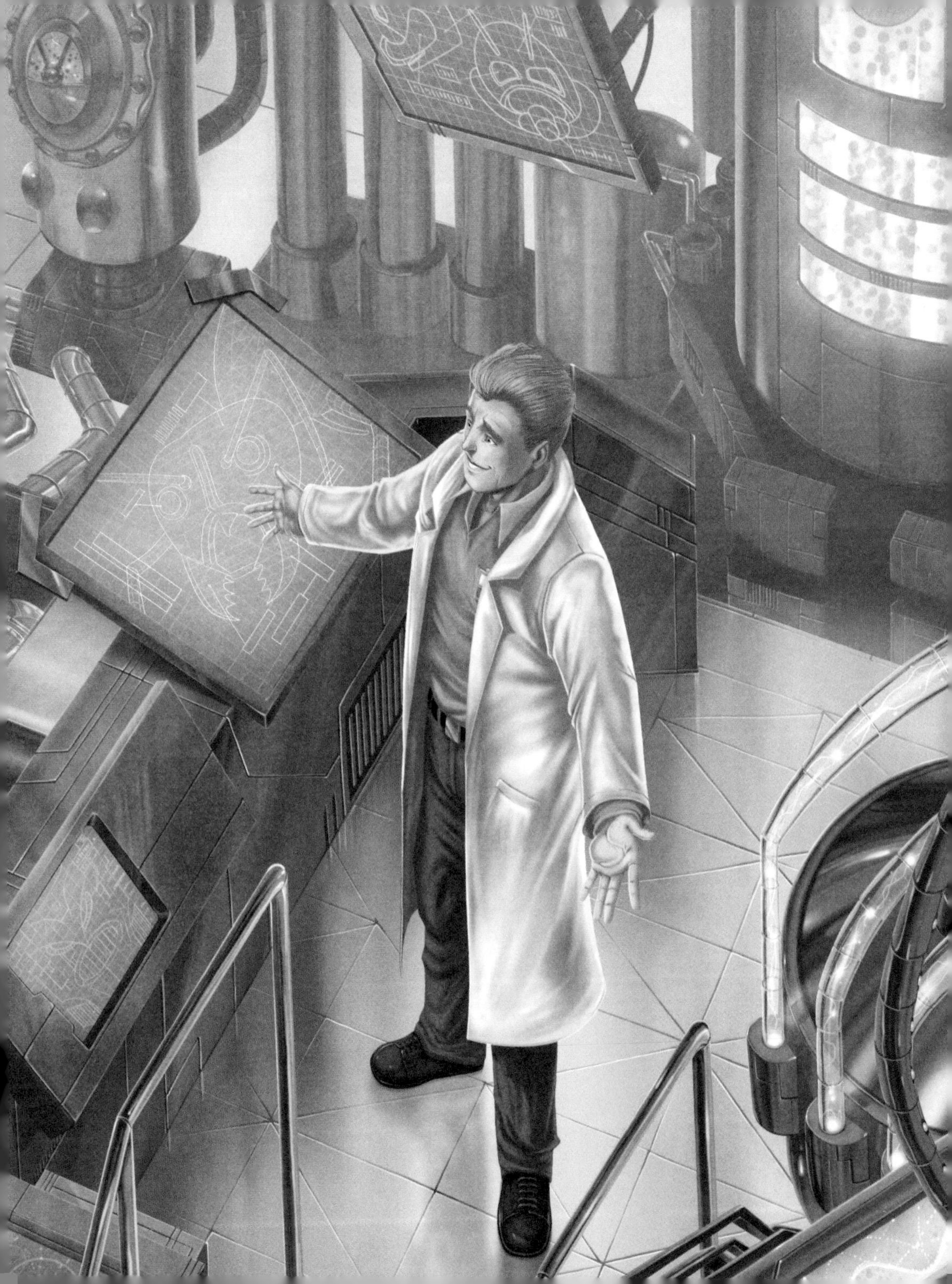

Whenever he is exposed to Dr. Pym's amazing Pym Particles, Scott Lang shrinks to only half an inch tall!

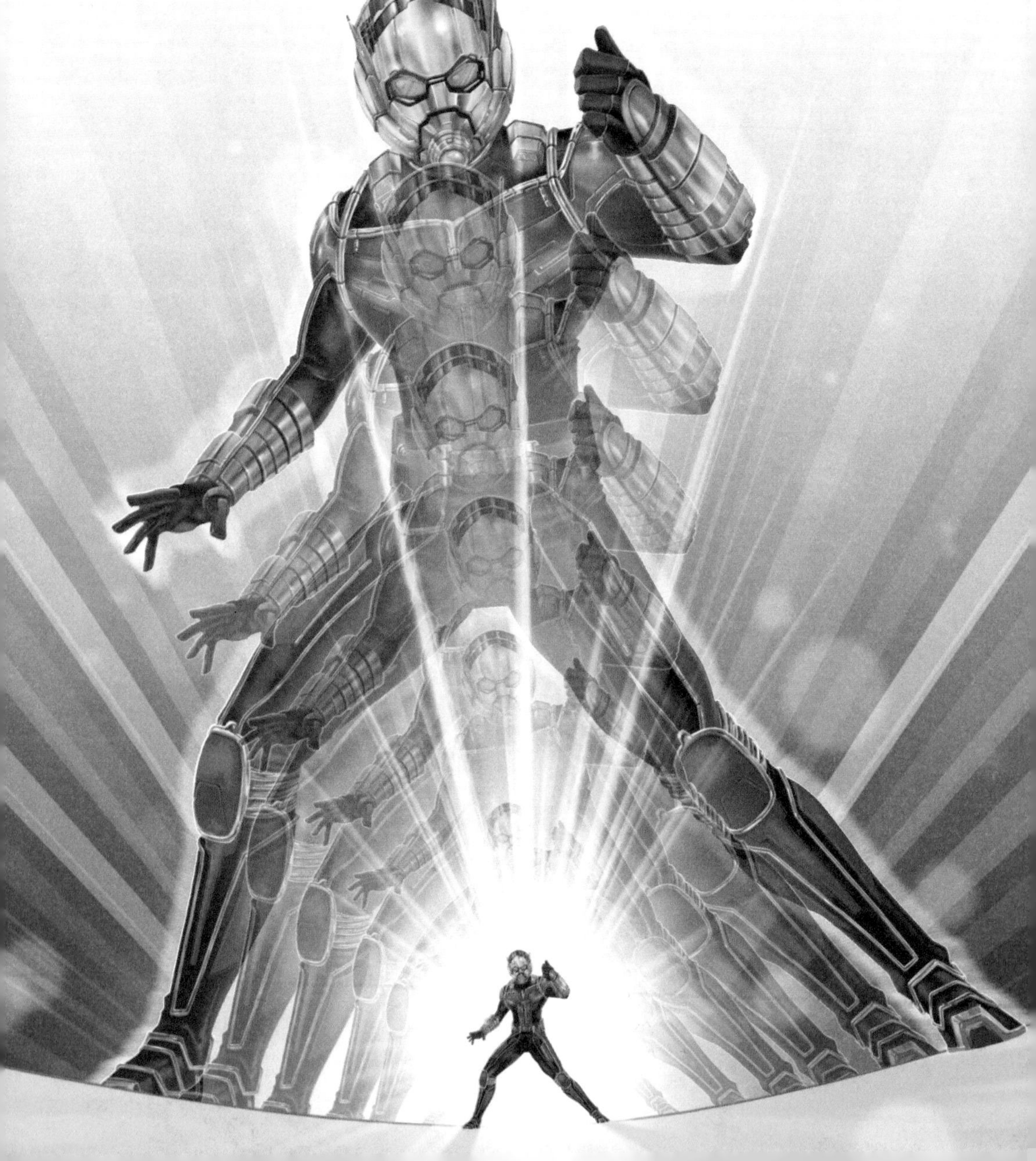

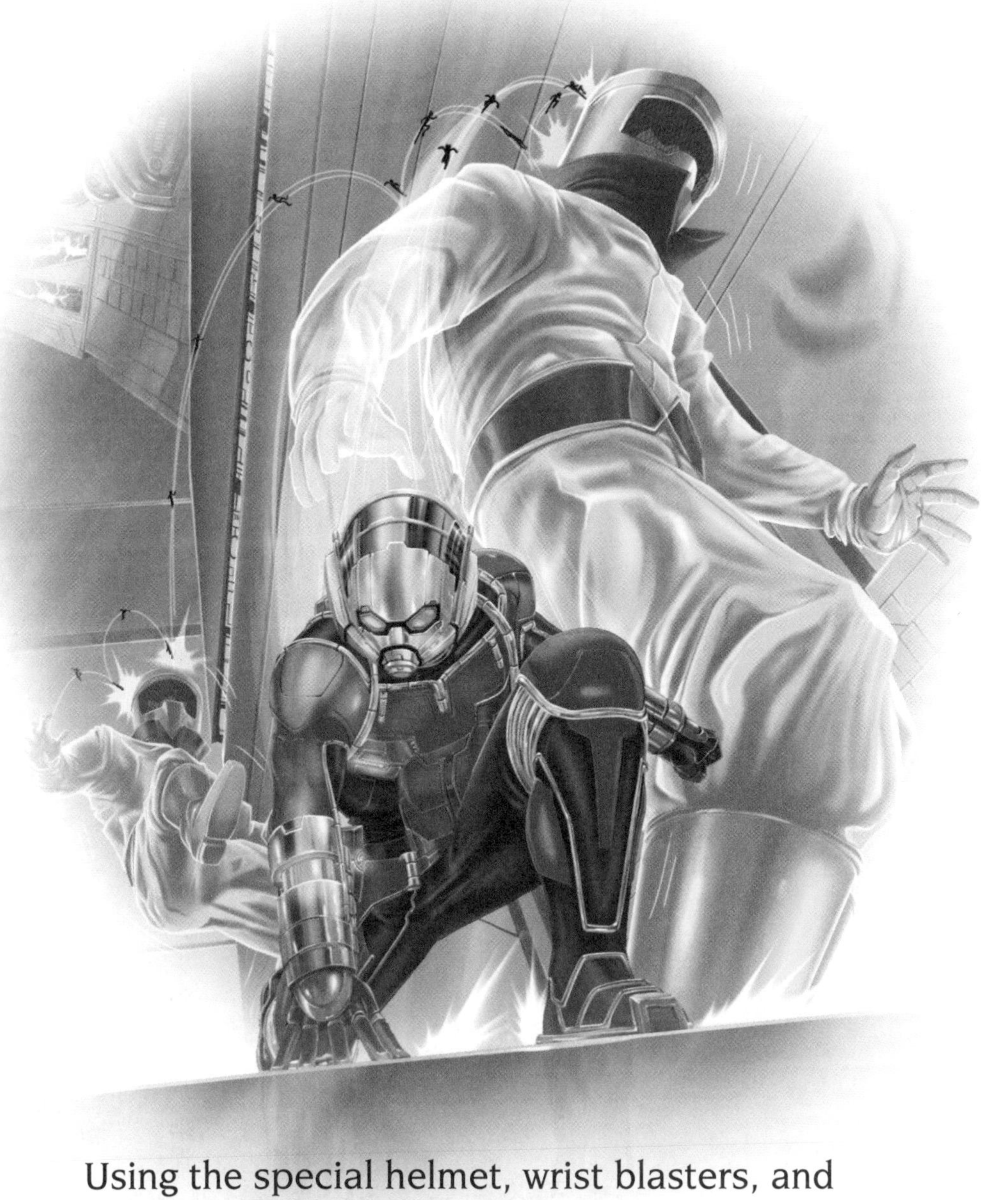

Using the special helmet, wrist blasters, and super-suit created by Dr. Pym, Lang goes into action as the ***ASTONISHING ANT-MAN***. There's no secret lair this tiny hero can't sneak into.

Even when he is small, Ant-Man has the strength of a full-grown man.

That can be quite a surprise for the bad guys!

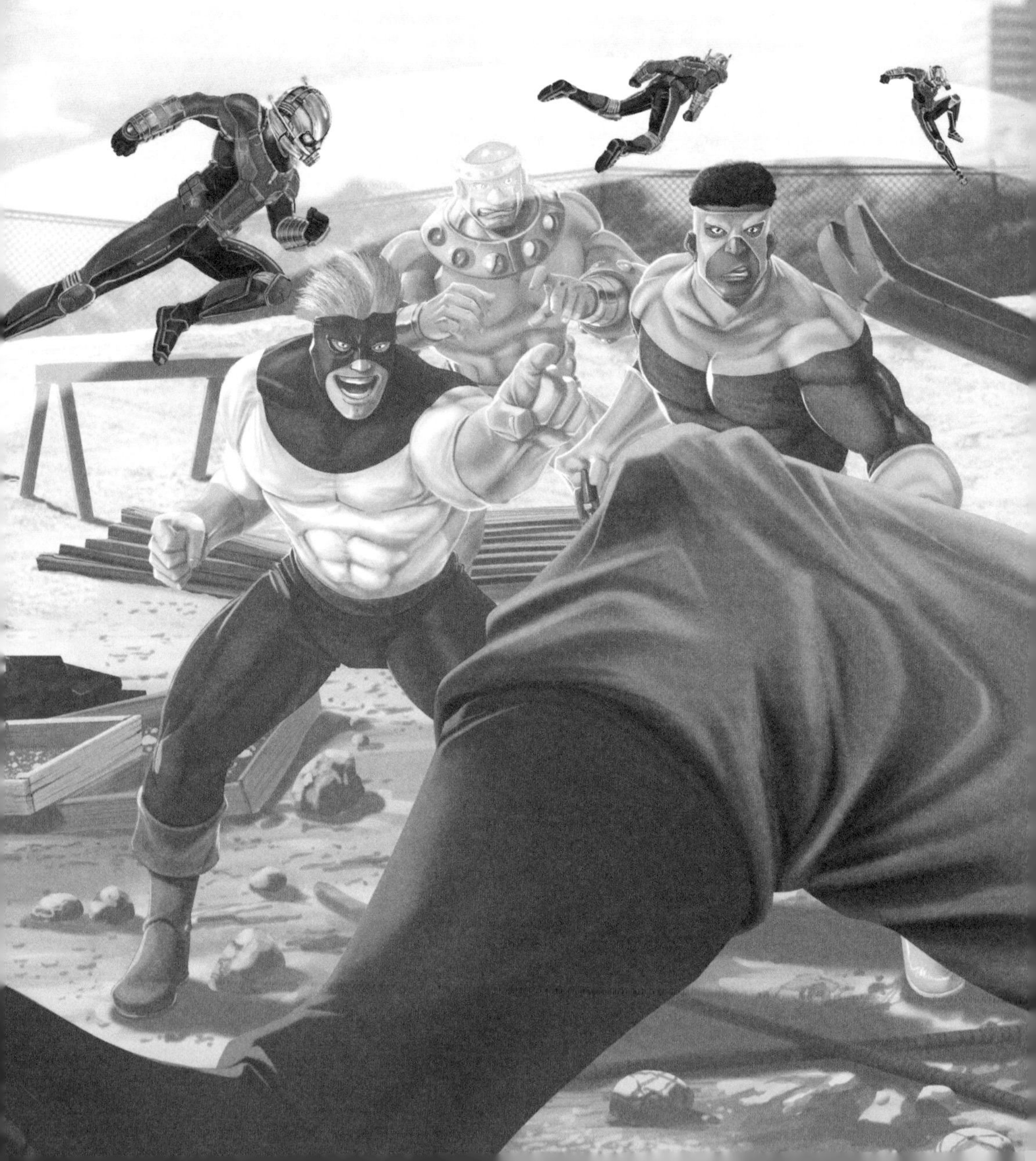

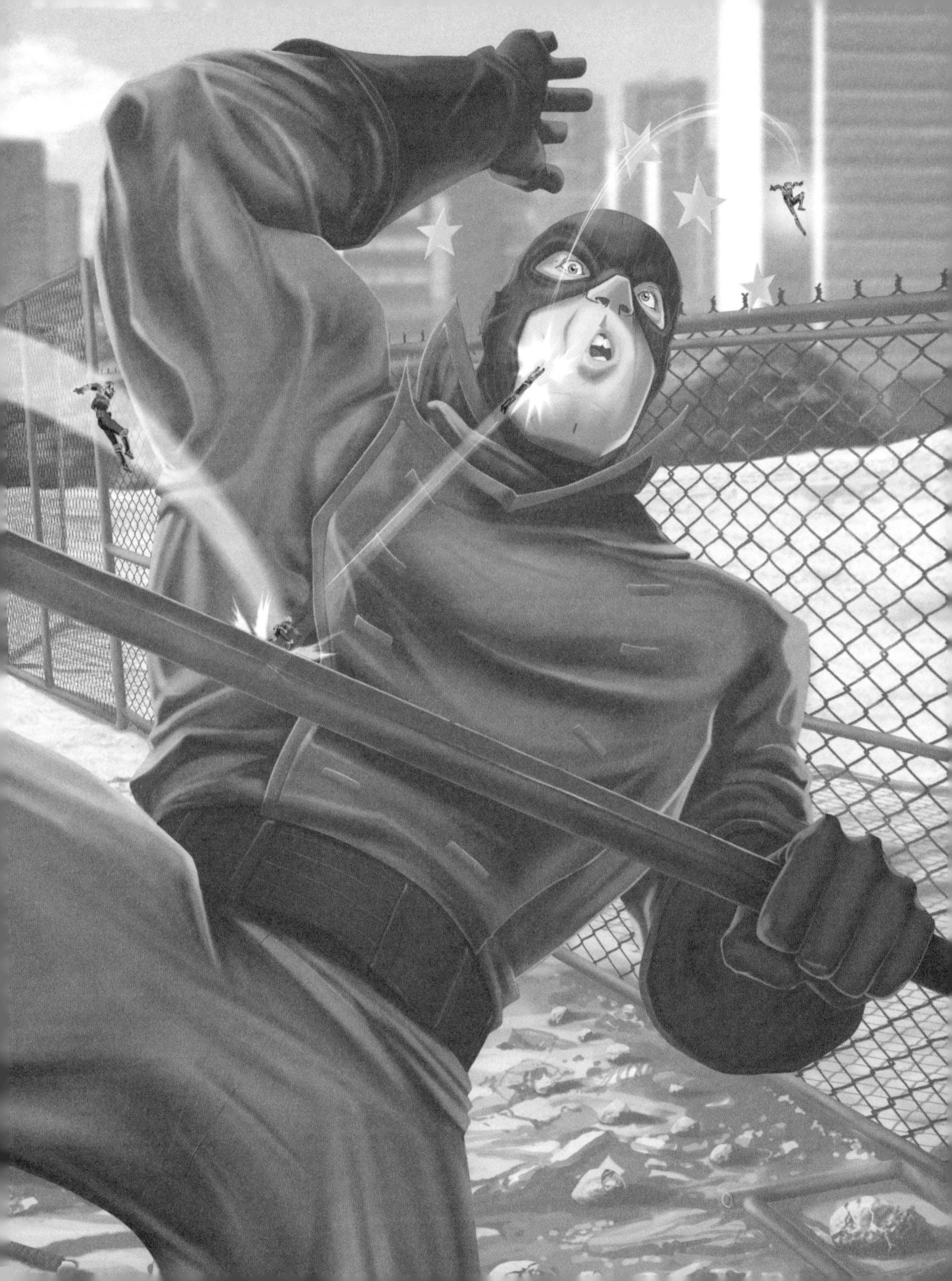

"Feel my sting!" Ant-Man shouts. He uses his wrist blasters to deliver powerful shocks.

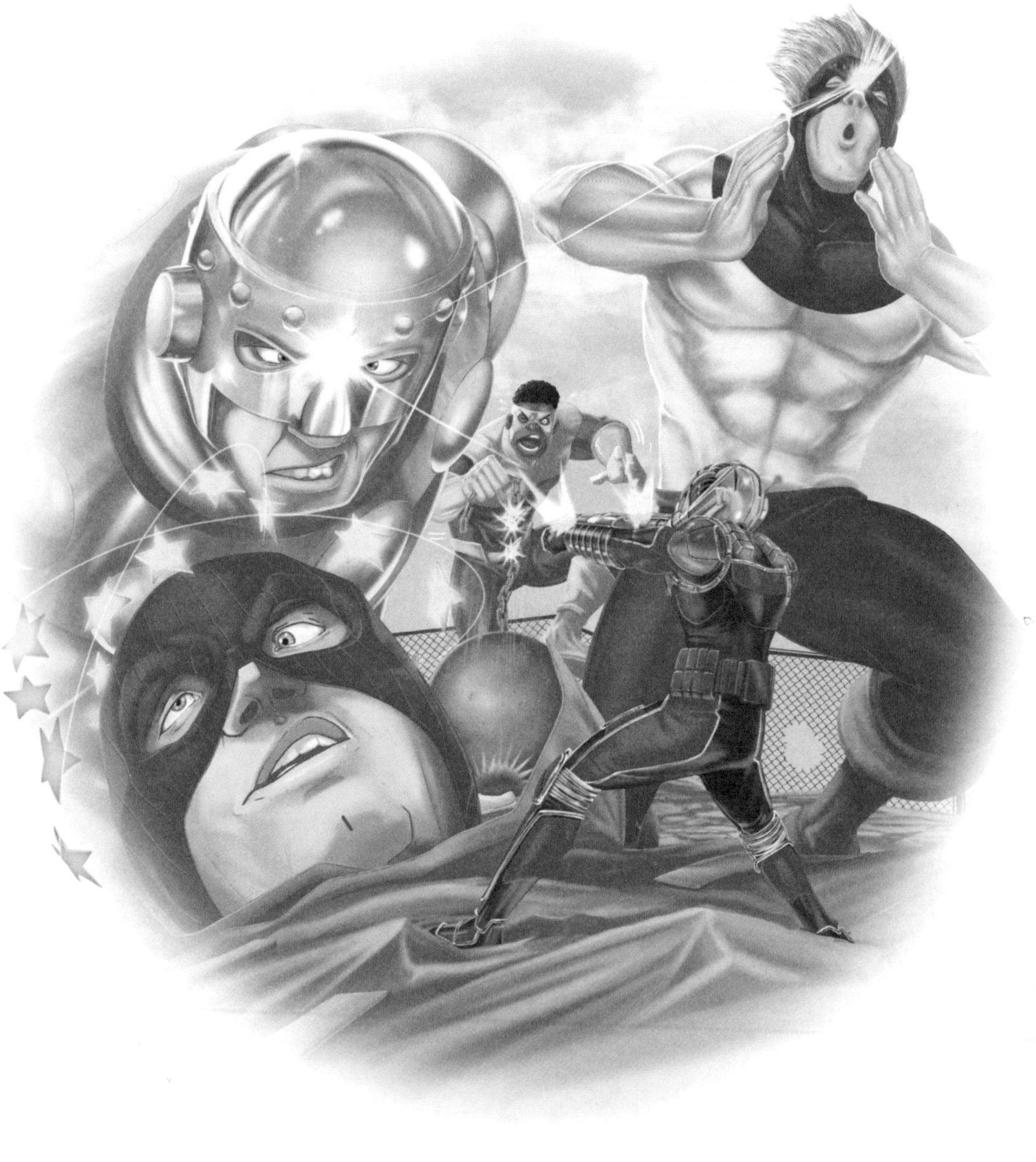

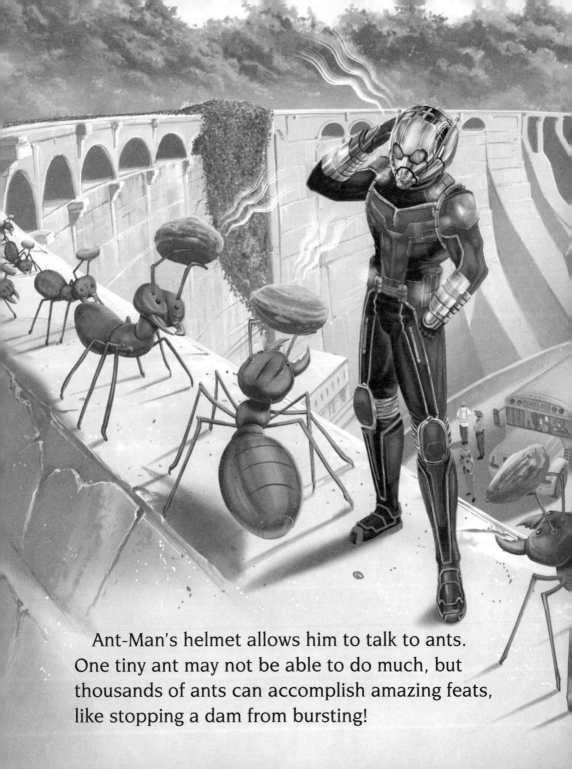

Ant-Man's helmet allows him to talk to ants. One tiny ant may not be able to do much, but thousands of ants can accomplish amazing feats, like stopping a dam from bursting!

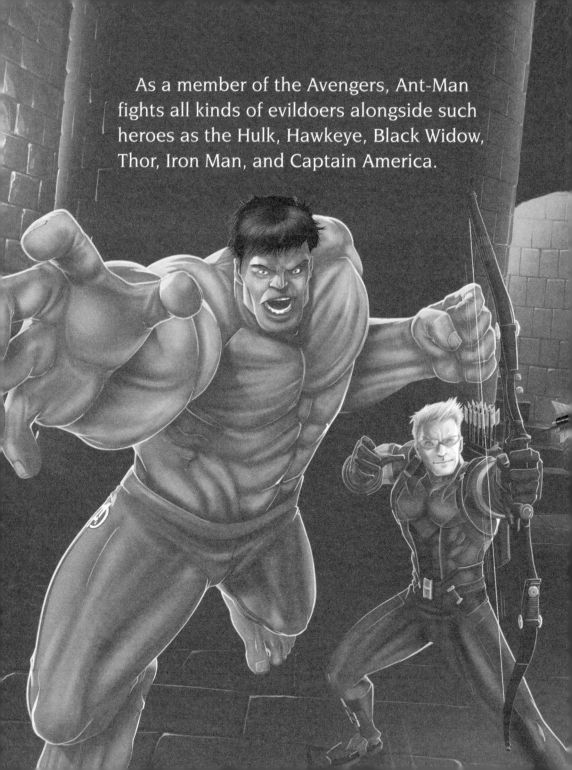

As a member of the Avengers, Ant-Man fights all kinds of evildoers alongside such heroes as the Hulk, Hawkeye, Black Widow, Thor, Iron Man, and Captain America.

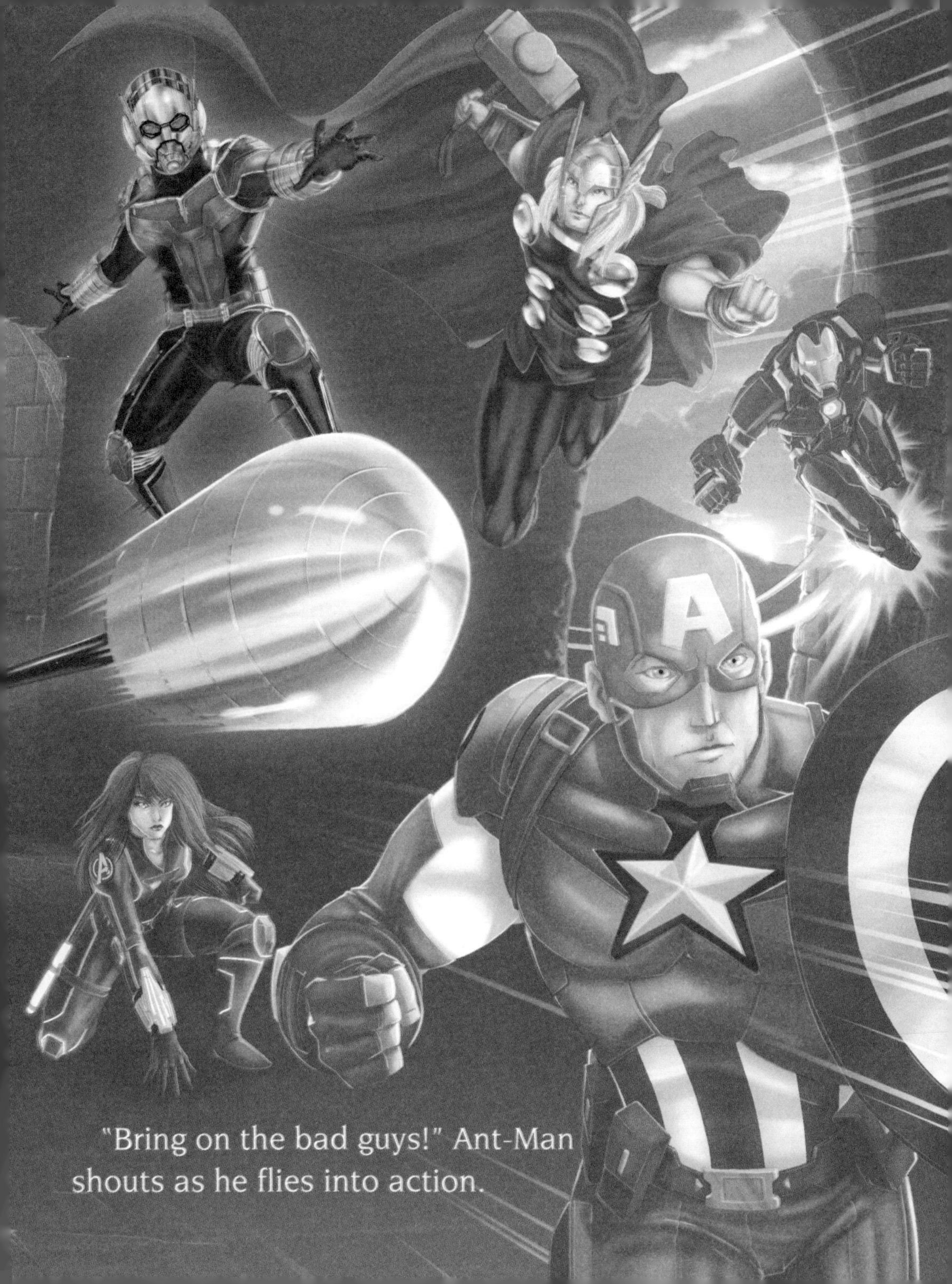

"Bring on the bad guys!" Ant-Man shouts as he flies into action.

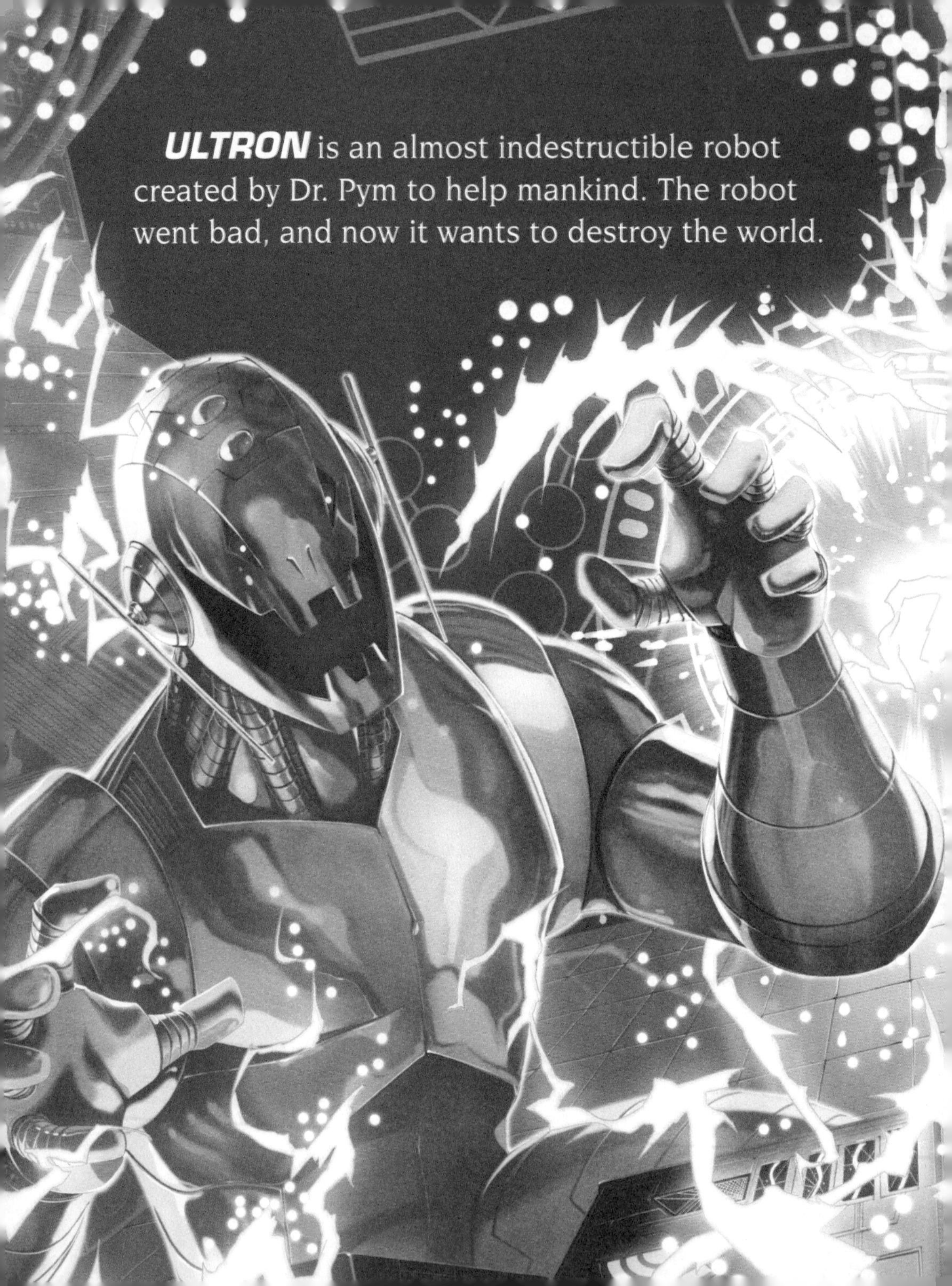

ULTRON is an almost indestructible robot created by Dr. Pym to help mankind. The robot went bad, and now it wants to destroy the world.

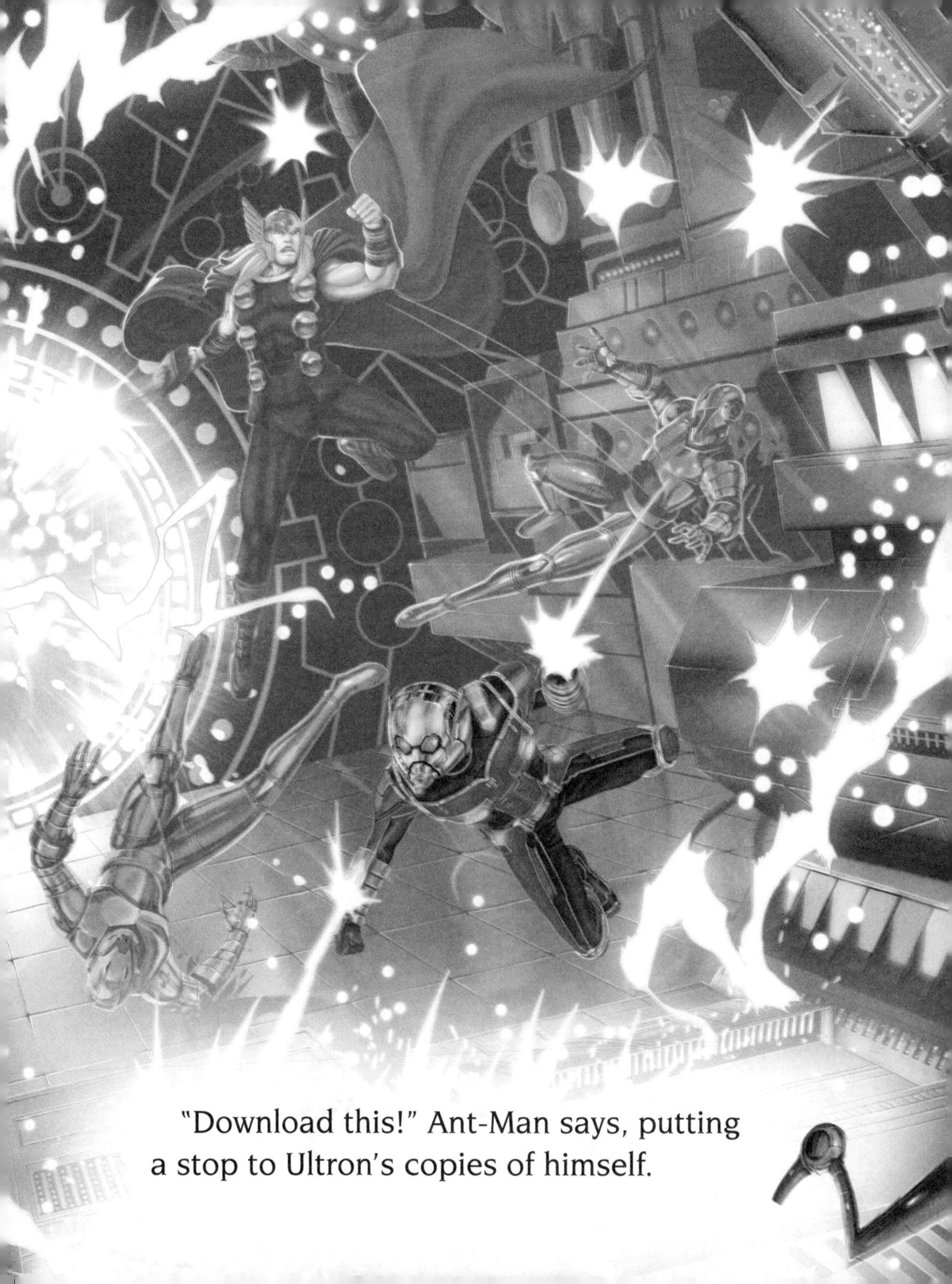

"Download this!" Ant-Man says, putting a stop to Ultron's copies of himself.

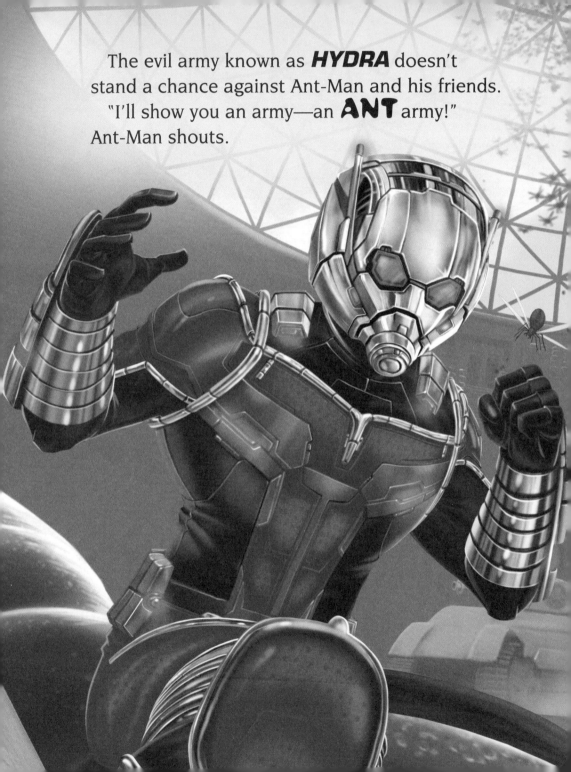

The evil army known as **HYDRA** doesn't stand a chance against Ant-Man and his friends. "I'll show you an army—an **ANT** army!" Ant-Man shouts.

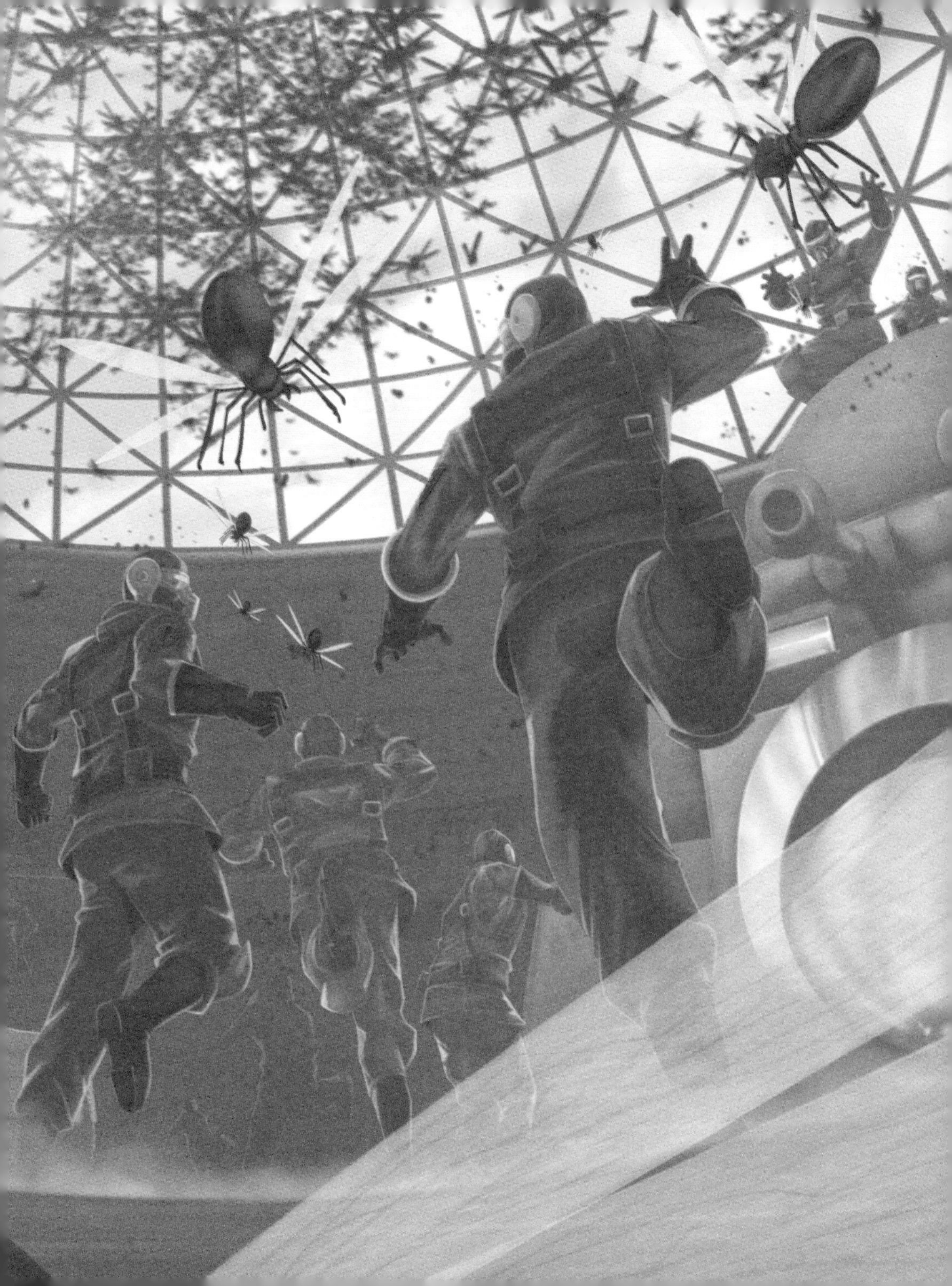

Sometimes it takes Ant-Man and all the Avengers to fight one villain, such as **COUNT NEFARIA**, who has many superpowers . . .

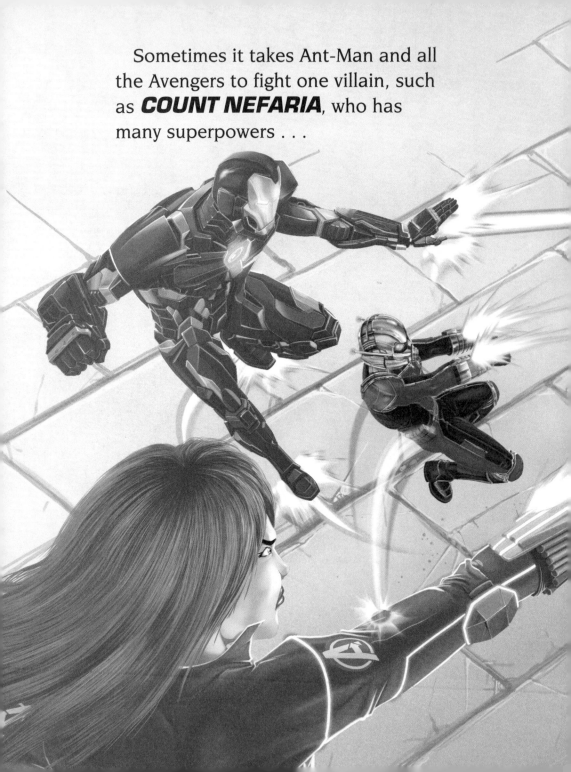

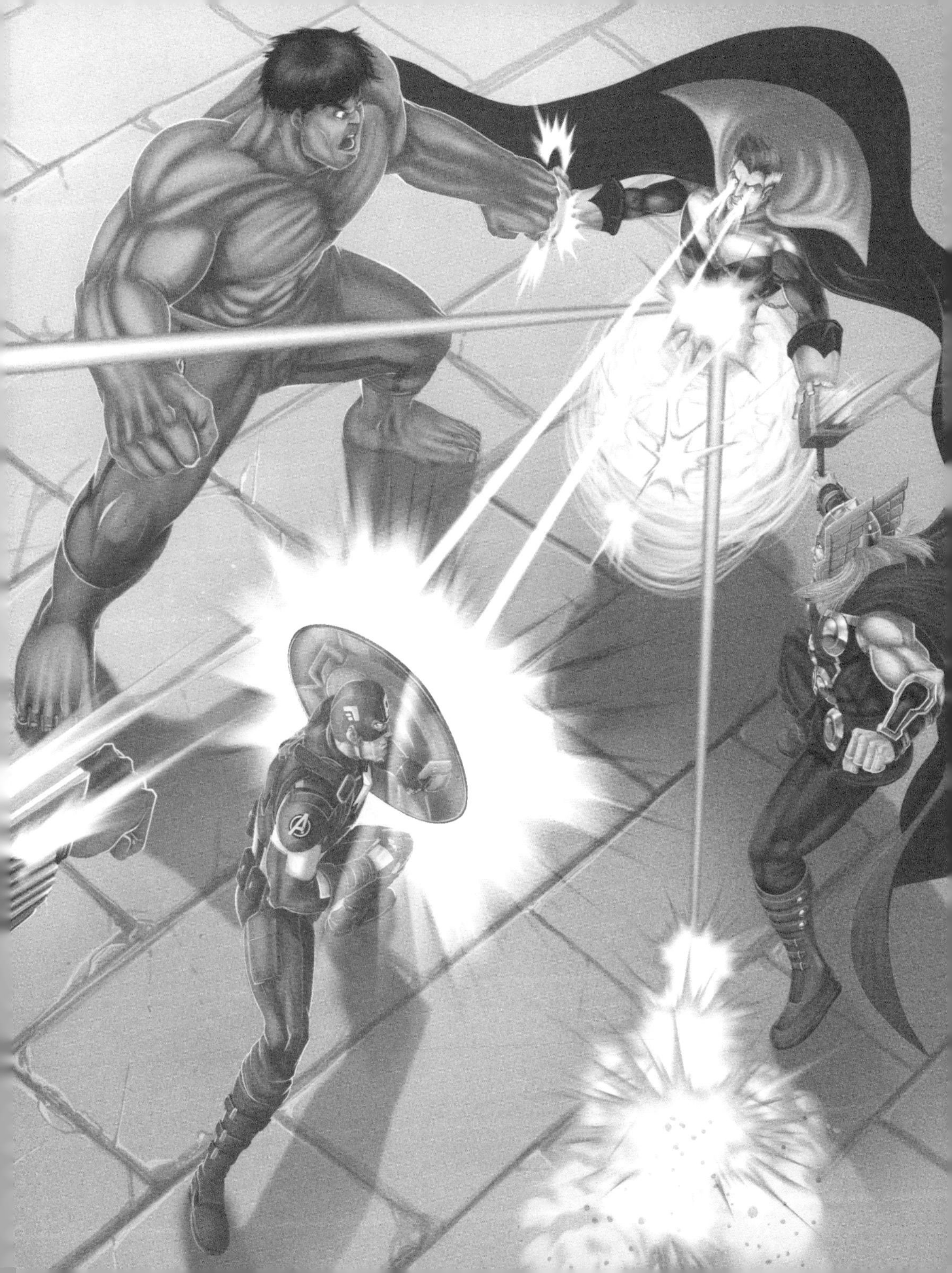

. . . and sometimes they fight whole teams of super villains, such as the ***MASTERS OF EVIL***, who combine their powers in hopes of defeating the heroes and taking over the world.

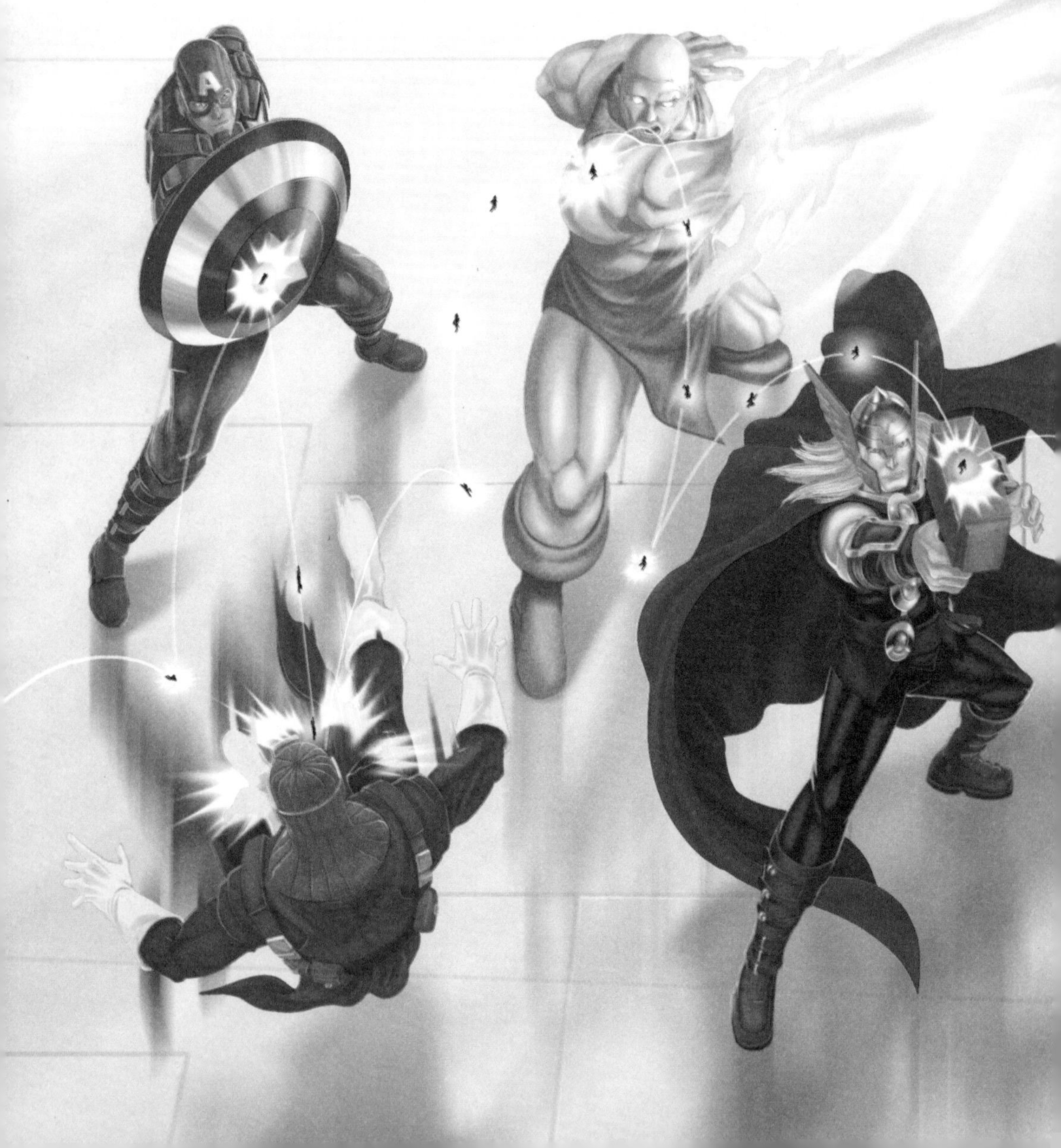

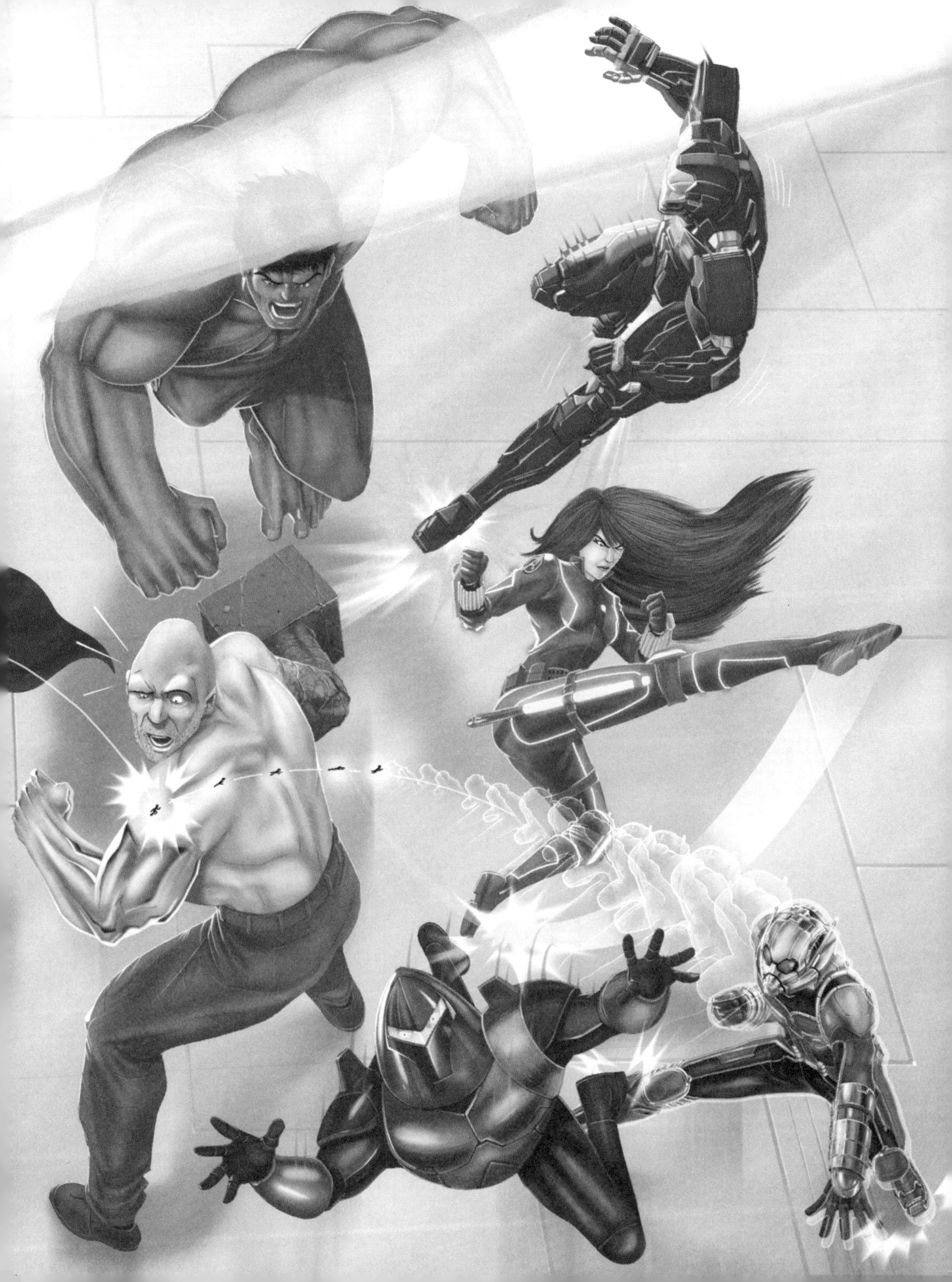

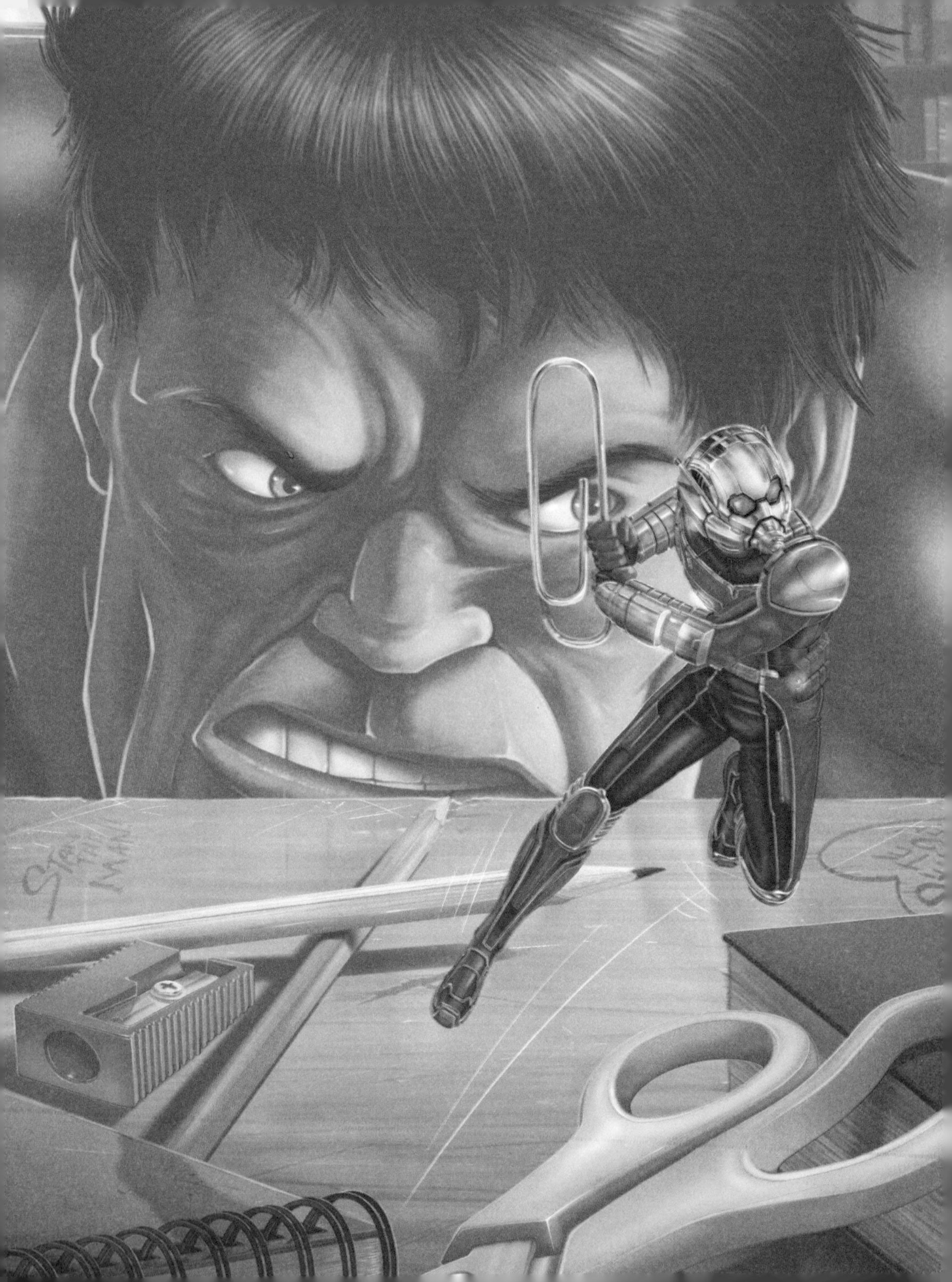

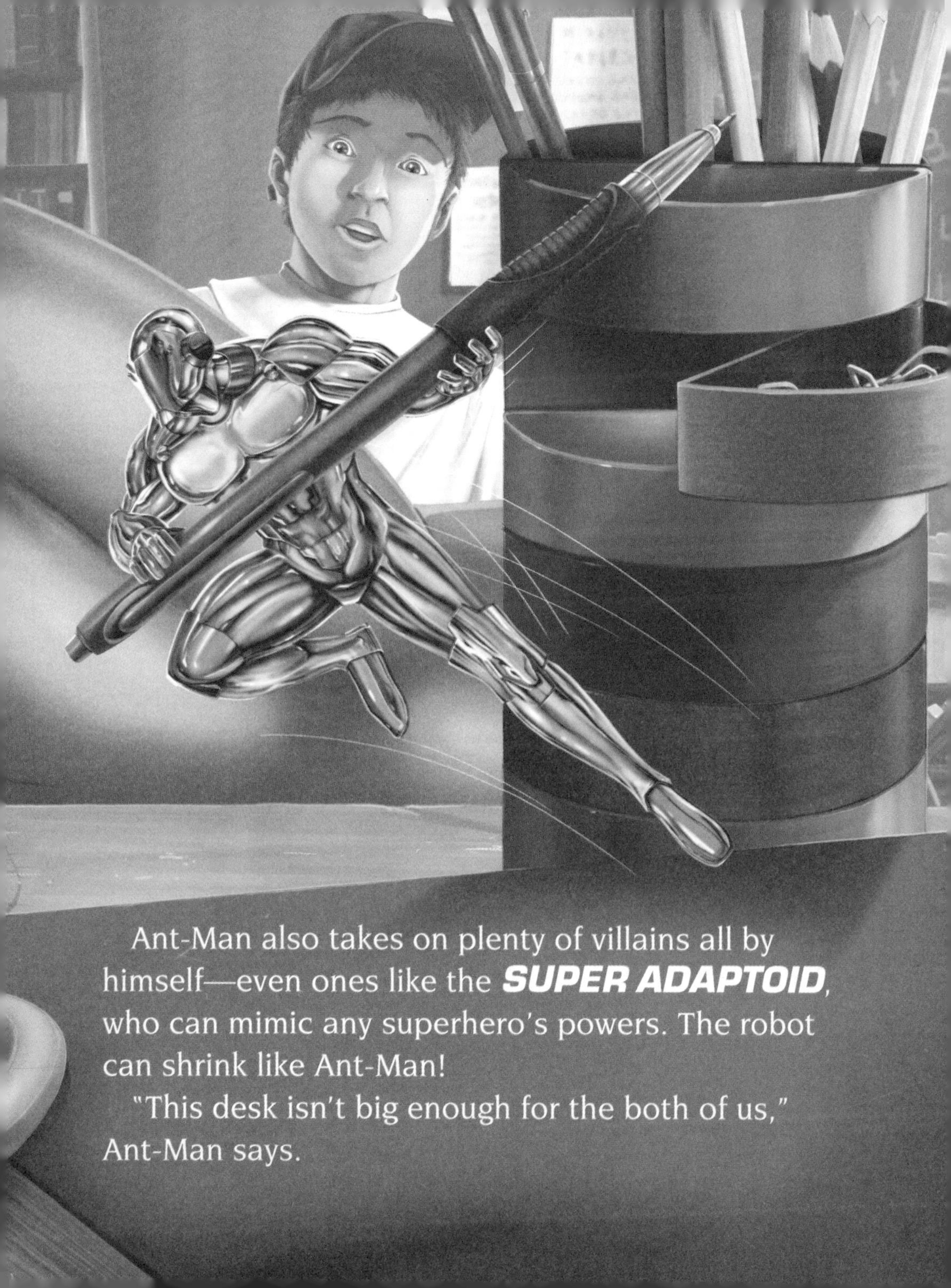

Ant-Man also takes on plenty of villains all by himself—even ones like the **SUPER ADAPTOID**, who can mimic any superhero's powers. The robot can shrink like Ant-Man!

"This desk isn't big enough for the both of us," Ant-Man says.

Big or small, everyone looks up to the little hero, Ant-Man!

GO, ANT-MAN!

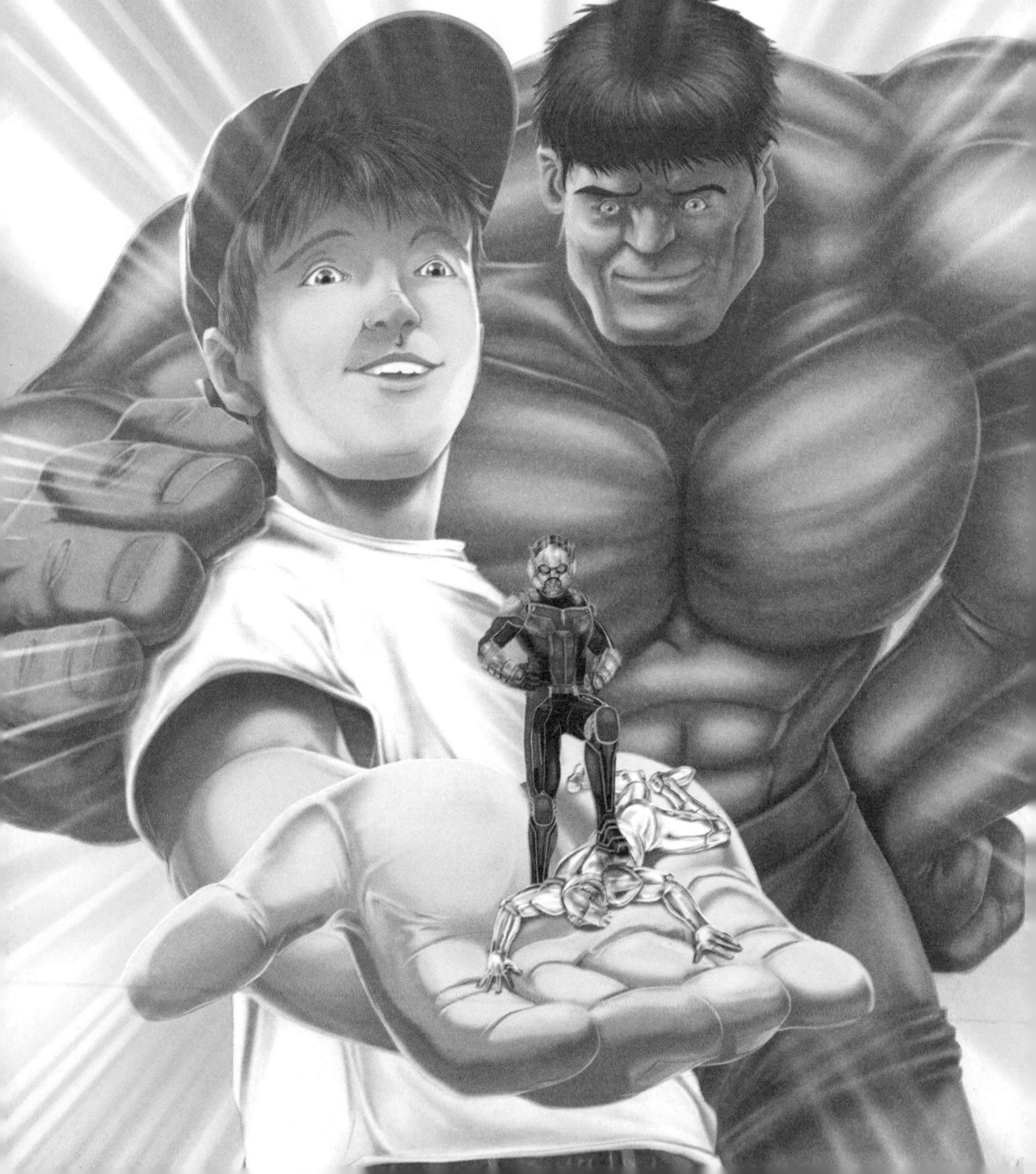